A Special Invitation

*T*o celebrate the season,
Queen Titania is hosting a
fancy-dress party on the mainland.
Lily has never been to the mainland.
None of the Bell sisters ever have –
except Tinker Bell, of course. And
a fancy-dress party too?
Why, Lily would give her wings
to attend!

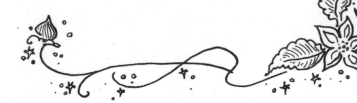

Other *Fairy Bell Sisters* stories:

The Fairy Bell Sisters

Lily and the Fancy-dress Party

First published in Great Britain by HarperCollins *Children's Books* in 2013
HarperCollins *Children's Books* is a division of HarperCollins*Publishers* Ltd,
77-85 Fulham Palace Road, Hammersmith, London, W6 8JB.

The HarperCollins website address is: www.harpercollins.co.uk

2

Text copyright © Margaret McNamara 2013
Illustrations copyright © Erica-Jane Waters 2013

ISBN 978-0-00-752070-1

Margaret McNamara and Erica-Jane Waters assert the moral right to be
identified as the author and illustrator of this work.

Printed and bound in England by Clays Ltd, St Ives plc

MIX
Paper from
responsible sources
FSC C007454

FSC™ is a non-profit international organisation established to promote
the responsible management of the world's forests. Products carrying the
FSC label are independently certified to assure consumers that they come
from forests that are managed to meet the social, economic and
ecological needs of present and future generations,
and other controlled sources.

Find out more about HarperCollins and the environment at
www.harpercollins.co.uk/green

For Isadora

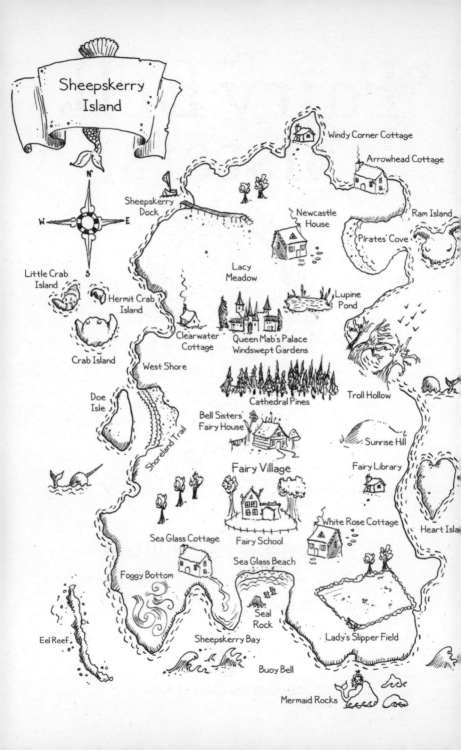

The Fairy Bell Sisters

Lily and the Fancy-dress Party

Margaret McNamara

Illustrations by Erica-Jane Waters

HarperCollins *Children's Books*

Chapter One

After the Summer People leave Sheepskerry Island and the asters show their pretty purple flower faces, the fairies know that autumn is hastening near. The days grow shorter and the shadows longer. A chill is in the island's evening air. The sugar maple trees begin to hint at the blazing colours to come, the smell of wood smoke is strong and the fairies put on gossamer shawls at night as they tell stories by the fire.

At the Fairy Bell house, Tinker Bell's little sisters – for that's who live there – were not enjoying the crisp autumn day. They were arguing. That didn't happen very often, as most of the time the sisters got along splendidly. This had started as a very happy discussion, about whose job it was to stack wood in the woodpile. But then it took a wrong turn into a small misunderstanding and from there it veered off towards bickering and now it was just short of an all-out fight.

I'm not fond of starting a story with a disagreement, so I think I'll stop for a moment to give the Fairy Bell sisters a few minutes to try to collect themselves and simmer down.

That will give us time, too, to make some introductions. If you haven't already met Tinker Bell's little sisters, their names are:

Clara Bell

Lily Bell

Rosie Bell

Silver Bell

Squeak

This story is about all the sisters, but it's mostly about Lily.

Lily Crystal Bell is a particular kind of fairy. She is probably the most like Tinker Bell of all the Bell sisters. Lily is headstrong and wilful and very stubborn. Like Tink, she always wants to get her own way. Some people may think Lily is a bit of a bossy-boots. But I don't think of her like that. Lily sees the world differently to other fairies. She notices small things that other fairies do not: the creamy shade of a hen's egg; the pattern of a spider's spots; a tiny glittering rock on

the beach. She may have trouble doing certain things – I'll tell you more about that very soon – but she knows what she's good at. That's what gives Lily her great confidence. She believes she's special. And she doesn't mind if other people believe it too.

You may be a bit worried to read a book about such a wilful, headstrong fairy.

But before you judge Lily too harshly, let me ask you this: have you ever wanted to shout out loud "I am so much *better* than anyone else! It is so wonderful to be *me*!"

If you believe that is an improper thing to do, or even to think about doing, I'm fairly certain you will not much care for this book. Off you go.

If, however, you're even a little bit like Lily, you might find it quite refreshing to read a book about a fairy who knows her own mind; a fairy who leaves her sisters behind to have an adventure on her own (an adventure that very nearly turns into a disaster). If that sounds like a good story to you, then please take the plunge and read on.

Chapter Two

*O*h, hooray! You plunged! How glad I
am.

Chapter Three

I may as well tell you what the Fairy
Bell sisters were fighting about before
we go much further. Autumn on
Sheepskerry Island is a time of bonfires
and long walks in the rustling leaves. It's
a time of change and a time to prepare
for winter. One of the Fairy Bell sisters'
big chores is to gather firewood from
the twigs and branches on the floor of
the Sheepskerry forests. It's hard work,

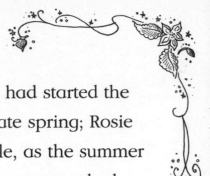

even with wings. Clara had started the woodpile back in the late spring; Rosie added to it, little by little, as the summer days went by; as autumn approached, Silver and her friend Poppy made a contest of it – who could gather the most, the quickest. (Silver, by three twigs.) And Squeakie was too young, of course, to do more than laugh as the woodpile grew.

And Lily? Well, so far Lily Bell had not done too much stick gathering, it must be said. Lily was good at avoiding work she did not like to do. What she most liked to do was to spend time experimenting with how she looked, which was what she was doing this crisp October morning.

"Honestly, Lily, you could help with this firewood at *some* point," said Silver from the front door of the Fairy Bell house. "I've done most of this week's gathering already." She stomped her feet on the doormat. "The rest is for you."

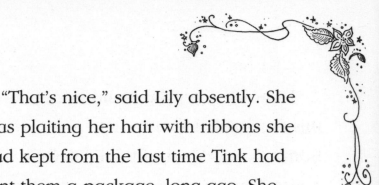

"That's nice," said Lily absently. She was plaiting her hair with ribbons she had kept from the last time Tink had sent them a package, long ago. She loved the look of the scarlet ribbons in her hair. She imagined they might have come from Peter Pan himself. "I'll do it later."

"That's what you said last week, Lily," said Silver. Her cheeks were red. "And you never got around to doing it."

"Well, it got done, didn't it?" asked Lily. She was trying to concentrate on her plaits. It was tricky to get them all even.

"That's because Rosie did it instead!" said Silver.

"I can't help it if Rosie wants to do my chores," said Lily.

"That's not the *point*!" said Silver.

"I didn't mind doing it," said Rosie.

"You see, she didn't mind," said Lily.

"You *always* get away with *everything*!" cried Silver. "You can't just sit there admiring yourself. You'd better help me right now."

"I'm not just admiring myself," said Lily. "I'm working on these ribbons!" The scarlet ribbon was far too long. She had to concentrate to cut it in just the right place. "I'll do it, but not right *now*."

"Clara!" cried Silver. "Make her do her chores!"

"Lily…" said Clara.

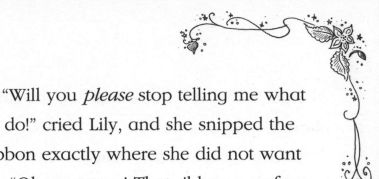

"Will you *please* stop telling me what to do!" cried Lily, and she snipped the ribbon exactly where she did not want to. "Oh no no no! That ribbon was from Tink! You made me ruin it!"

Squeak squeaked.

"*You* ruined it, not me!" cried Silver.

Lily's eyes filled with tears. Her lovely moment thinking about Tink and Peter Pan had been spoiled. She turned to face her sisters. "All we do on this island is work, work, work. It's not enough that we have to make our own beds and wash our own clothes and fetch the water from the pump. And go to school. And put up with all the boring Sheepskerry fairies." Even as Lily said

all this, she knew she was going too far. But once she got started, she couldn't stop. "But now it's getting to be winter, and the work will triple and it will be freezing cold and dark and *miserable*."

"Oh, Lily," said Rosie.

Lily brushed Rosie and her sympathy away. She threw the scarlet ribbon into the fire.

"Lily! Don't!" cried Clara.

"Sometimes I just want to leave you all and never come back," said Lily. Her voice was hoarse.

She flew to the doorway and put on her boots in a fury.

"Lily, no!"

But Lily paid Rosie no attention.

22

"I hope you're happy now, Silver," she said. Then she flew out into the cold, slamming the door behind her.

Chapter Four

*T*hings can get a bit dramatic among sisters.

By lunchtime, Lily had come home. She had even calmed down enough to exchange two words with Silver over lunch. "Butter?" said Lily.

"Thanks," said Silver.

By teatime, Lily and Rosie were out in Lady's Slipper Field, watching for deer. And when the sun went down that evening, the sisters were cosy by the fireplace (made with wood gathered by Lily), listening to Clara as she read from their favourite story.

"'Her voice was so low that at first he could not make out what she said,'" Clara read. Clara had reached one of the most exciting parts of *Peter Pan*:

the moment when their big sister Tink was in the most danger. Even Squeak was perfectly quiet as Clara continued. "'Then he made it out. She was saying that she thought she could get well again if children believed in fairies.'"

They all knew what would happen next (perhaps you do too), but still it took four mugs of warm milk – and one bottle – for them all to recover from such a dramatic moment in the story. Once they had settled down, Lily volunteered to tuck Squeak into her cot in the great room, for it was way past her bedtime. Lily got the blankets just right. Squeakie's tired eyes opened for a moment.

26

"*Ma-bo-bo*," said Squeak.

"I love you too, Squeakie," whispered Lily.

Just before bed, Rosie handed Lily her scarlet ribbons. "They're a little charred from the fire," she said. "But I know you'll find a use for them." Clara looked on and smiled.

Lily took them from Rosie gratefully. "Sorry about all that," whispered Lily.

"It's all right," said Clara and Rosie, at the same time.

"Time for bed," said Silver. She gave

Lily a quick hug. Lily hugged her back.

And the Fairy Bell sisters were at peace again.

Chapter Five

*T*he next morning was a school day. Lily left the Fairy Bell house a little early, for today was her special time with her teacher. She dressed and was out of the fairy house before the sun had fully risen.

As early as it was, there was a smiling fairy teacher to

greet Lily at the door.

"Hi, Faith!" said Lily. Faith was one of the Learned sisters, all of whom were teachers. Lily gave Faith a hug. She loved their special time together.

"Good morning, dear Lily," said Faith. "Come, sit down and let's read together."

Now one thing you might not know about Lily Bell is that she was not much of a reader. Lily loved stories – hearing them read out loud and making them up herself – but she struggled with making sense of words on the page. Sometimes words jumbled together. Sometimes they blurred. Sometimes they even jumped from one place on a page to another. Imagine how hard it was to read

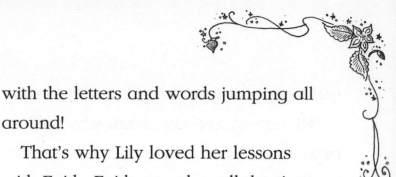

with the letters and words jumping all
around!

That's why Lily loved her lessons
with Faith. Faith gave her all the time
she needed to read and write. Like her
sisters, Patience and Fortitude, Faith was
a wonderful teacher.

Lily read out loud for a bit from a
book that Faith had made especially for
her. (Lily had decorated it with her own
pictures.)

"'Her godmother then touched her
with her wand,'" Lily read slowly, "'and
at the same instant, her clothes turned
into cloth of gold and silver, all beset
with jewels.'"

"Nice job, Lily!" said Faith.

"I love that story," said Lily.

"What progress you've made!" Faith said. "You must have been working hard."

"I *have* been working hard," said Lily. "Even if my sisters think I haven't."

"Sisters can be a trial," said Faith. "Though I do envy you, that you have so many of them. I'm quite lonely here at the schoolhouse, now that Patience and Fortitude have left for the Outer Islands."

Faith's two sisters had been teachers on Sheepskerry for many fairy years. But the Outer Islands needed good teachers too and Faith's sisters had left in the summer to teach the young fairies there.

"How I would love a little

companionship, now that winter is
drawing near." Faith sighed, and
then shook her head as if she'd been
somewhere far away. "But there's no
help for that. I shouldn't complain. I
have all my fairy students as family."

33

She went out to the front porch of the fairy schoolhouse and rang the bell. "And here they come now!"

With a flutter of dozens of wings, the fairies of Sheepskerry Island flew into fairy school. All the fairies learned together and learned from one another.

Just as Faith was about to clap her hands to start their day, she was interrupted by the distant call of a conch shell.

"That's Queen Mab's clarion!" cried Faith. "It sounds as if she's on her way here! Fairies, on your best behaviour, please!"

All the fairy students were amazed.

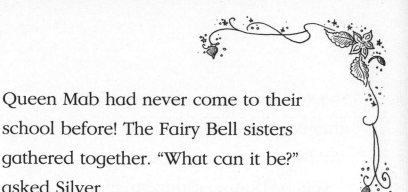

Queen Mab had never come to their
school before! The Fairy Bell sisters
gathered together. "What can it be?"
asked Silver.

"I have no idea," said Lily. But she
noticed her wings were trembling.

Queen Mab flew to the front of the
classroom. "I hope you will forgive this
interruption, Faith Learned," she said.

"Of course, my queen!" said Faith,
curtseying low.

Queen Mab smiled. "My beloved fairy
family," she said, her voice low. "I've
had word from my dear friend on the
mainland, Queen Titania."

"I hope it's not bad news," whispered
Clara.

Lily's wings quivered again. "I don't think so," she said.

"To celebrate the season and to bring joy to the long autumn nights, Queen Titania is hosting a fancy-dress party on the mainland."

"The mainland?" said Lily. Her heart skipped a beat. She had never been to the mainland. None of the Bell sisters ever had – except Tinker Bell, of course. It was three days' flight from Sheepskerry, too long and too dangerous a journey for young fairies. Lily kept her wings as still as she could. A fancy-dress party on the mainland? Why, she would give her *wings* to attend!

"A fancy-dress party," whispered

Poppy Flower to her best friend, Silver. "What's that?"

"It's a dressing-up party," said Silver. "You know, with costumes."

"Ooh!" said Poppy. "I love to dress up!"

Lily did not say a word. She was the best at dressing-up on the whole island. Everyone knew that.

"Just one fairy from each island may attend the fancy-dress party," said Queen Mab. Then she peered out and looked right at the Fairy Bell sisters. Quietly, she said to them, "Queen Titania hasn't yet learned the lesson you taught us, Silver, at the Fairy Ball."

Silver blushed.

Queen Mab's voice grew loud again. "There will be a prize for the best costume in Fairyland. And Queen Titania has asked us to send one fairy from Sheepskerry to take part."

"Ooh, Lily," said Rosie. "No wonder your wings were quivering. You should go."

Lily held her breath.

"I'd like you all to think who would create a costume that will make Sheepskerry proud," said Queen Mab. "I would rather show pride in our fairy island than win, as I'm sure you know."

Queen Mab paused for a bit, to let the fairies talk among themselves. The Cobweb sisters knitted the best shawls

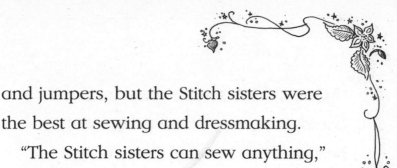

and jumpers, but the Stitch sisters were the best at sewing and dressmaking.

"The Stitch sisters can sew anything," said Acorn Oak. "I think one of them should go."

The three Stitch Sisters – Fern, Satin and Feather – put their heads together.

"They sew so beautifully," said Poppy. "In a way, it's right that one of them should go."

"But in a way it's not," said Clara. "We all know that Lily would be the best at making a costume. But we must let the fairies decide. That's the Fairy Way."

Fern Stitch flew straight up to Queen Mab. The Fairy Bell sisters could not hear what she was saying, but later they heard about the conversation from Iris Flower, who heard it from Sugar Bakewell. "It's true, we are known far and wide for our tiny stitching and intricate patterns," Fern had told the queen. "But all three of us think someone else should go to the mainland. Someone else who will make the best costume in the land."

As soon as Fern stepped away from Queen Mab, there was a murmuring in the crowd, as if all the fairies were speaking with one voice. At first it sounded like they were saying, "*Li! Li!*" But then Clara and Rosie and Silver – and, of course, Lily – heard more clearly what their fairy friends were saying.

"*Li-ly! Li-ly!*" came the cheer.

"Listen!" said Clara.

"I'm listening!" cried Lily.

"LI-LY! LI-LY! LI-LY!"

41

"Lily Bell, please come up before me," said Queen Mab.

Lily flew over in a rush. Her wings had stopped trembling now.

On her way she turned to the Stitch sisters. "Oh, Fern, are you very sure?" asked Lily. "Would you really give up your place for me?"

"Of course I would," said Fern Stitch. "I don't really want to go to the mainland. Not that much anyway."

"Besides, it's awfully hard work making a costume," said Feather.

"Oh, thank you!" said Lily, giving them a huge smile. Then she curtsied to Queen Mab, just as her teacher had. "And I most humbly thank you, Queen

42

Mab," she said.

"Don't thank me," said Queen Mab. "Thank your fairy friends."

Lily looked out at the happy faces of her sisters and her schoolmates.

"Oh, I will make you proud, Sheepskerry fairies!" she cried. "I will make Sheepskerry Island very proud indeed!"

Chapter Six

*T*he next day was misty and grey, but Lily's mood was the complete opposite. She dressed before dawn in a little travelling outfit: a royal-blue suit with pink polka-dot edging. And matching polka-dot shoes.

Lily had hardly slept a wink all night. Queen Mab had given her instructions about what to do on the mainland and her head was swimming. Lily would

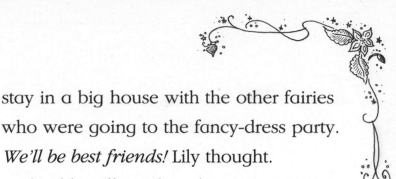

stay in a big house with the other fairies who were going to the fancy-dress party. *We'll be best friends!* Lily thought.

She'd be allowed to choose seven items from Queen Titania's Magical Costume Trunk and from those she would put together her costume. The costume was to be based on a theme chosen by the queen.

Please let Queen Titania choose a good theme for the costumes! Lily thought. *I don't want to dress as a piece of fruit!* That idea alone kept her up for an hour. Then she spent a long time picturing herself on a mainland street, lightly flying next to two or three mainland fairies who had become her close friends. She imagined the cheers as she entered the fancy-dress party in her gorgeous attire.

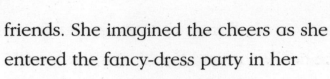

Lily regarded her sweet little suit in her full-length mirror. She tied a navy-blue ribbon in her hair. *Nice!* she thought. Unfortunately, the ferry ride would be cold and wet, so she'd also have to wear a hefty oilskin coat to keep warm and dry.

"My yellow coat?" Lily asked her reflection in the mirror. "Or the green one?"

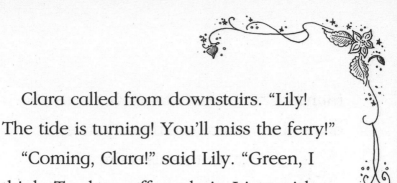

Clara called from downstairs. "Lily! The tide is turning! You'll miss the ferry!"

"Coming, Clara!" said Lily. "Green, I think. To show off my hair. I just wish it wouldn't frizz so in this weather!" She leaned down to pick up her luggage – three large bags full to bursting. (One was only for shoes.) She could barely carry them all.

"Silver! Rosie! Can you help me with my bags?"

Rosie flew up the stairs. "Oh my goodness, Lily!" she said. "Do you really need to take that much? It's just for the weekend."

"I'm sure most fairies could get along without very many clothing choices,"

said Lily. "But I cannot. Not to mention shoes. Oh, where are those little dancing shoes I like so much? Can I fit them in?"

"There won't be dancing at the party, I don't think," said Rosie. "So you could leave your dancing shoes at home. And isn't that *my* green coat?"

"I thought you'd want me to have it for the weekend, Rosie. It looks so good on me on a rainy day like this."

Lily hoped Rosie would say yes, and she did, with a smile.

"Come on, Lily," said Silver. "The ferry won't wait."

And in a moment the bags were gathered and all five Fairy Bell sisters were out of the door. They flew down

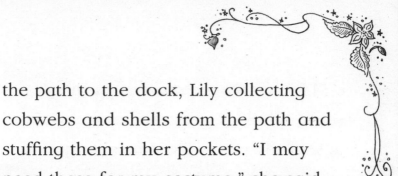

the path to the dock, Lily collecting cobwebs and shells from the path and stuffing them in her pockets. "I may need these for my costume," she said. Clara carried Squeak in her arms as she hurried Lily along. Just before they got to the dock, Squeak looked at Lily with her big brown eyes. "*Doh-ca!*" she said.

"There, there, little Squeak," said Lily. "I can't possibly take you to the mainland. You'll go when you're a grown-up fairy, like I am."

"Don't you wish, just a little bit, that we were all going together?" asked Silver. "I don't much care about the mainland, but we're always—"

"I know. We are *always* together," said Lily. "But I can't just be on this tiny little island all my life. I need to get out and spread my wings."

"Of course you do, Lily," said Clara. "We all want to grow up." Lily thought she noticed a catch in Clara's voice. "This is your turn to shine."

They heard a splashing in the water.

"There's Merryweather!" cried Silver.

Merryweather was an unusual ferry. She wasn't a boat at all; she was a grey seal who stopped by Sheepskerry once a month to take fairies on the long trip to the mainland. I don't know if you've ever seen seals swimming, but they look rather like dogs when they're paddling. They

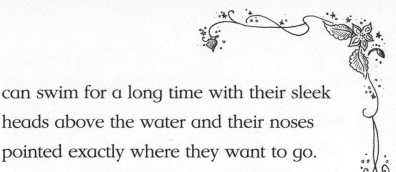

can swim for a long time with their sleek heads above the water and their noses pointed exactly where they want to go.

Merryweather gave three hoarse barks.

"That's the signal," said Clara. "Time for you to get on, Lily."

Lily turned to say her goodbyes. "Bye-bye, little Squeakie," she said. She held Squeak close. "I wonder how much you'll change while I'm gone."

"Goodbye, Lily!" cried Rosie. "I know you'll do beautifully. Take good care of yourself! And say hello to Lulu if you see her on the mainland!"

"I will!" said Lily. Lulu was Rosie's friend – a human child. Human people

made Lily a little nervous, but how
lovely it would be to see Lulu again!

"We'll be here on the dock waiting
when you come back," said Clara.

Lily flew over to Merryweather's grey
head and settled comfortably in the
seal's sleek fur. Her luggage just fitted,
even if it might get a little wet.

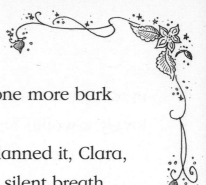

Merryweather gave one more bark and paddled away.

And as if they had planned it, Clara, Rosie and Silver took a silent breath together and sang in harmony.

The water is wide;
You'll soon pass o'er.
And then you'll find
A land a-new.
Sheepskerry's strength
Will give you hope,
Till you return,
Our sister true.

Lily looked out to the distant horizon. Then she turned and waved once more to her sisters on the dock. "At last," Lily said to herself. "I'm Lily Crystal Bell. And I'm on my own."

Chapter Seven

"There she is! There she is!" Lily heard the calls even before Merryweather was at the mainland ferry station.

Three very beautiful and very elegantly dressed fairies were waving a greeting. Lily started to wave back – but then she realised they weren't waving at her. She lowered her hand.

"I don't mind," said Lily to Merryweather. "I'm going to be fine here."

But as Lily looked around at the unfamiliar setting, her courage failed her for a moment.

The mainland was very different from Sheepskerry.

There were no human people in sight, which was a relief, but Lily had never seen so many fairies. Not at the Fairy Ball; not at Queen Mab's island meetings; not even in her dreams. How could there be so many fairies in one place? She gave Merryweather a quick kiss (that was her payment!) and unsteadily flew down the gangplank to the fairy town.

Lily saw fairies of every age and shape and size. They were all in a

terrible hurry. And if they noticed Lily Bell at all, it was only to tell her to get out of the way.

But oh, what an extraordinary place this was!

Buildings crowded the streets – not just fairy houses for one family, but gigantic fairy houses that must have fitted a dozen or a score or a hundred fairies all together. The fairy houses were so high they seemed to reach almost to the sky. Instead of trees and flowers, there were long roads and pigeon buses. And looming up above the town were two enormous buildings. Lily could read their big signs – one was the Museum of Fairy History; the other,

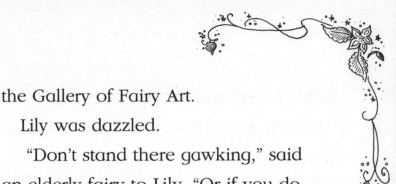

the Gallery of Fairy Art.

Lily was dazzled.

"Don't stand there gawking," said
an elderly fairy to Lily. "Or if you do,
at least move out of the way so an old
fairy like me can get by."

"Oh, of course," said Lily. "May I ask,
do you know the way to—"

But before Lily could finish her question,
the elderly fairy had flown away.

How does anyone find her way here?
Lily thought. But then she remembered
the instructions Queen Mab had given
her. A fairy named Avery would greet
her at the ferry dock and then take
her to stay with two mainland fairies,
Claudine and Amanda Townley. *One*

thing at a time, Lily thought.

"Avery, Avery. Where is she?" said Lily. She half wished she could squeeze Rosie's hand right now or that Clara would take charge. She was even feeling that sometimes she was a little too harsh with Silver—

"Lily? Lily Bell of Sheepskerry?"

"Yes, that's me."

"I'm Avery Pastel, Claudine and Amanda's serving fairy." Avery was neat and pretty, and she smiled at Lily shyly. "Welcome to the mainland."

"I'm very pleased to meet you, Avery," said Lily.

"Let me take those," said Avery. She picked up two of Lily's bags.

"Oh, thank you so much," said Lily.
"They're very heavy."

Avery looked startled. "You don't
have to thank me," she said. "I'm a
serving fairy." She led Lily to an elegant
carriage. "You sit here," she said, settling
Lily into a comfortable seat. Then Avery
took a seat on a bench at the back of
the carriage. "To the town house!" she
said to the carriage driver, a bright-eyed
sparrow. And off they flew.

As the two fairies made their way
over the tall buildings in the afternoon
sun, Lily and Avery chatted about
the mainland and what life was like
here. "We don't have serving fairies on
Sheepskerry," Lily said.

Avery was so startled she almost
bounced right off her bench. "No
serving fairies?" she said. "How do you
manage?"

"We do a lot of things for ourselves,"

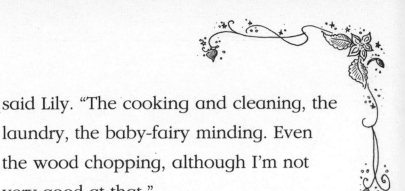

said Lily. "The cooking and cleaning, the laundry, the baby-fairy minding. Even the wood chopping, although I'm not very good at that."

"The serving fairies take care of that kind of thing here. Fairies like you – they don't have to lift a wing."

"Oh, how marvellous!" sang Lily. If she had been paying attention, she might have seen that Avery's face fell a little. "I could get used to this!"

Chapter Eight

When Avery and Lily arrived at
the Townley sisters' house, Lily was
exhausted from her journey, but not
exhausted enough to miss out on any
detail. "A crystal chandelier!" she cried.
"And look at this staircase! It curves!"
Lily imagined herself floating slowly
down the staircase with her fancy-dress
costume on. She imagined the other
fairies looking at her with wonder and

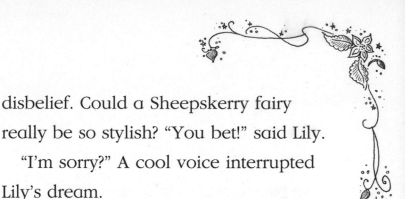

disbelief. Could a Sheepskerry fairy really be so stylish? "You bet!" said Lily.

"I'm sorry?" A cool voice interrupted Lily's dream.

Lily spun around to find two very pretty and very fashionable fairies staring at her. "Oh, no, I'm sorry!" Lily said. "I was thinking out loud!" Her face turned pink. "I'm Lily Bell, from—"

"Oh yes, we know where you're from," said one of the fairies. "You're from—" and she paused; Lily thought she heard a little sniff, "Sheepskerry Island. I suppose you're a shepherdess?"

The other pretty fairy giggled.

"No, there aren't sheep there any more," said Lily. She thought the fairies

were teasing her, but she couldn't tell.

"Um... are you Amanda and Claudine?" Lily asked.

The two fairies looked down their pert little noses. "Who else would we be?" said the taller one. "I'm Claudine. Amanda and I own this house. Queen Titania has made us host all *twelve* fairies for the fancy-dress party. From the mainland *and* the islands."

"Avery, take her coat, please," said Claudine. "How quaint it is too," she added quietly, but not so quietly that Lily did not hear. Lily was glad she had worn her little blue suit as her arrival outfit. *They can't make fun of this*, she thought.

"It's very kind of you to have invited
us all to stay with you," said Lily, using
her best manners, even though the
Townley sisters were being not so polite

themselves. "I adore your house," she said. "It is so elegant! And so huge! You must love living here."

"*Humph!*" said Amanda. "I suppose you haven't seen many *real* fairy houses before."

"I've seen almost all the houses on Sheepskerry, plus the summer cottages," said Lily. "So I think I do know pretty well what a fairy house looks like."

Amanda and Claudine smiled. "Not a *mainland* fairy house," said Amanda.

Then they turned to go. "We will see you at dinner," said Claudine. "That will give you time to change—" she paused, and arched an eyebrow, "into something suitable."

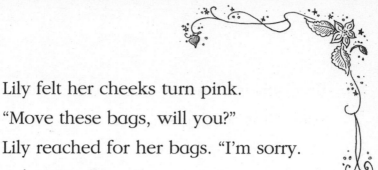

Lily felt her cheeks turn pink.

"Move these bags, will you?"

Lily reached for her bags. "I'm sorry. Are they in your—"

"Please, Lily. Avery carries bags here," said Amanda.

"I'll just take these upstairs," said Avery to Lily. Then she whispered, "Never mind them. Not all mainland fairies are so snobby. Come on up with me. I'll get you settled in."

Chapter Nine

*T*he sting of Claudine and Amanda's unfriendly greeting felt less keen as Lily looked in wonder at the bedroom where she was to stay. Instead of curtains made of oak leaves, there were delicate water-silk panels of shell pink. A sweet gold-and-white dressing table – with a three-way mirror! – was nestled in a corner. A plush rose carpet was on the floor. And the bed! Lily flew over and fell on to the pillowy feather duvet. "There's nothing like this on Sheepskerry!" she said.

"It's nice, isn't it," said Avery without even looking around. "I'll leave you now so you can have a moment's peace before dinner."

"That sounds good," said Lily. "Will you sit next to me at the dinner table, Avery? I have to admit I'm a little nervous around those Townley sisters."

Avery shook her head. "Oh, no!" she said. "I never sit at the table, especially not on a grand occasion like this! Why, there must be a dozen fairies staying here at least! I'll eat with Caraway Cooke in the kitchen after you've had your meal."

Lily's face fell. The mainland kept surprising her.

"Will there be anything else, miss?" asked Avery.

"Please, call me Lily!"

Avery smiled a cautious smile. "Will there be anything else, Lily?" she asked.

"There is one thing." Lily wanted to ask why the Townley sisters seemed so… unfriendly. But she didn't want Avery to think she couldn't handle herself on the mainland.

"If you're wondering why Amanda and Claudine are so unfriendly," said Avery, "the reason is that the Townley sisters win the fancy-dress prize every single year. All the mainland fairies seem to think that's the way it *has* to be." Avery busied herself by unpacking Lily's bags. "But now the island fairies have been invited and Amanda and Claudine have heard that island fairies are very good at creating things out of bits and pieces. Especially you."

"Oh my!" said Lily.

"And that's why they are *not* on their best behaviour." The little porcelain clock on the mantelpiece struck five. "Now I must fly," said Avery. She slipped out of the door and Lily was on her own.

"I'd better change into a different dress," said Lily to herself. "Which means I'll have to re-do my nails too. I hope I'll be fancy enough for dinner!"

As she got ready, Lily thought a lot

about what Avery had told her. *How nice that people are saying I'm good at creating things!* she thought. *But how sorry I am that Claudine and Amanda are cross about it.*

When she was dressed and her nails were drying, Lily flew over to the window to get a breath of fresh autumn air. She looked out on the city below her. "What a lot of lights!" she said. Lily gazed up at the stars, but she couldn't make them out for the bright city glow.

Then she strained her eyes towards the harbour to see if she could glimpse the ocean or the islands beyond. She could not. "Oh well," said Lily, with a small sigh. "I know they're home and safe on Sheepskerry."

I'm sure you can guess who was on Lily's mind!

Chapter Ten

*D*inner that night was not so bad. The food was delicious and the conversation was lively. All the other fairies – even the ones from the mainland – were perfectly nice. Fawn Deere, from Doe Island, seemed almost like a friend. Avery was so busy serving that Lily hardly caught a glimpse of her, but when she did they exchanged smiles. If Claudine and Amanda hadn't made

their guests feel so nervous, Lily and the visiting fairies might have had a lovely time.

After dinner, when she went up to her bedroom, Lily was so exhausted from her long day that she fell asleep the moment she sank down into her pillows. She didn't hear the noise of carriages and the murmur of voices and the whir of fairy wings passing her windows all night long. She slept soundly and dreamed of seals, fir trees and a large bag with wings.

In the morning she woke early. On Sheepskerry she always rose with the sun and she could not change her habits in one day. Not to mention that the

fancy-dress party was this very evening!
How could anyone sleep!

Lily dressed quickly – for her – in a
floaty little high-waisted dress with a
lovely print of crimson poppies. And red
boots. She swept her hair into a high
ponytail, hastily made up her bed and
decided to go downstairs to explore. "I'll
make myself some breakfast before they
wake up," she said to herself.

The big, long hallway was silent and
still. Lily crept past the closed doors of
Claudine's bedroom and Amanda's and
found her way down the stairs. The
Townley dining room was empty. Nor
was there anyone in the parlour, though
a fire was burning brightly. "Aha!" said

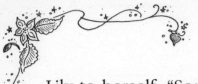

Lily to herself. "Someone's been up and about."

She hadn't noticed it last night at supper, but there was a little doorway off to the side of the dining room. She opened it carefully. It led to a wide stairway and Lily heard the clatter of the kitchen at the base of it. *So that's where the food comes from*, she thought. *I thought it was magic!*

The kitchen was a hive of activity. There was a fairy cook with an open, cheerful face. *She must be Caraway,* thought Lily. Next to her flitted another fairy, but she was working so quickly Lily could hardly tell who it was. Then she realised—

"Avery!" she said.

"Oh my goodness, miss! What are you doing here? All the fairies are asleep."

"No, they're not," said Lily. "You're a fairy and you're up and working away. What can I do to help?"

"I'm Caraway Cooke," said the older fairy. "And since you're here, keep yourself out of the way. You modern fairies don't know how to do much of anything, anyway. Not like my dear sister, Saffron, though of course there's no room for her in *this* house." Avery waggled her eyebrows at Lily at that remark. "Avery, tend that fire. It's not hot enough for me to put the scones in."

"But I'm squeezing the oranges—"

"Then hurry up about it, please." Caraway Cooke was not unkind, but she was very, very firm. She pointed to

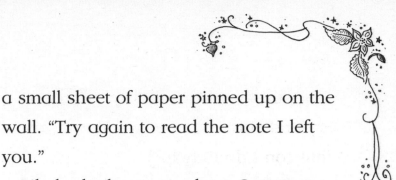

a small sheet of paper pinned up on the wall. "Try again to read the note I left you."

Lily looked over to where Caraway Cooke was pointing. There was a long list pinned to a corkboard. The writing was tiny, but there were funny little doodles drawn all over it.

Avery flew over to consult the list of jobs for the day. She stared at it for a long time.

Lily flew over to her side.

"I like the drawings," said Lily. "Did you do those?"

Avery nodded. "I like to draw," she said. She was staring at the list. "Could you just… read it to me?"

Sweep Floor

Mop Floor

Polish shoes + boots

Water plants

Hang out the washing

Lily could tell it was hard for her to ask. She smiled. "I'm not very good at reading," she said.

Caraway Cooke dropped a spoon. Avery's wings nearly stopped.

"Not very good at reading?" said Avery. "Then why aren't you a—"

"Who's not very good at reading?" Claudine's voice cut through the kitchen. She was floating at the top of the stairs.

"I'm—" Lily began.

"Um, what she *means*," Avery said quickly, "is she's not going to make a big fuss about *my* reading trouble. Breakfast will be along in just a few more minutes."

"See that it is," said Claudine. "Lily, you should be upstairs. This way, please."

"I'm coming," said Lily, but she stayed right where she was. Claudine did not look happy.

85

"What was all that about?" asked Lily when Claudine had shut the door. "Why can't I say that I'm—"

"Don't you know?" asked Avery.

"Know what?" asked Lily.

"Don't you know," said Caraway Cooke very quietly, "that fairies who aren't good at reading or numbers become serving fairies here on the mainland?"

She put the scones in the oven and closed the door fiercely. "I'm a cook because I'm a Cooke sister and it's what I love to do. I'd very much like to have my younger sister working here too, but the Townley fairies prefer Avery – she comes cheap."

Caraway wiped her hands on her apron. "Avery's drawings should be in the Gallery of Fairy Art, but she has such trouble reading, don't you, Avery?" Caraway looked at her with great tenderness. "I do my best here, but I'm no teacher. And she has no sisters to help her. She has no one at all."

Chapter Eleven

*B*efore we go any further, I think I'd better tell you how it is that Avery had no fairy sisters and Lily had so many. It's no secret that a fairy is born when a human child laughs for the first time. The Fairy Bell sisters were born of a particularly happy child; Becca was her name, and she had a bright, musical laugh. Baby Becca laughed for the first time one morning in the music room of

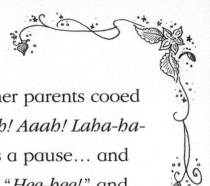

her family's house as her parents cooed over her. *"Ha-hah! Hah! Aaah! Laha-ha-ha! Ho-ho!"* There was a pause… and then she giggled a last *"Hee-hee!"* and finally she took a breath. (It was a big laugh for a first timer.)

Becca's *"Hah-hah!"* became Tink; the second *"Hah!"* was Clara. *"Aaah!"* was Rosie, *"Laha-ha-ha!"* was Lily, *"Ho-ho!"*

was Silver, and that last *"Hee-hee!"* was, of course, baby Squeak.

The Fairy Bell sisters had a happy birth indeed!

But some fairies have a different beginning. Occasionally, a very sullen child manages a first laugh late in life. *"Humph! Hamph!"* Usually such a child is not laughing in delight, but laughing at another's misfortune. From that sort of laugh, very unpleasant fairies are born. (Claudine and Amanda were surely the products of a *"Humph! Hamph!"*)

Avery was born of a very happy human child called Emma, who managed to laugh earlier than all the other babies, but didn't quite recognise

90

what she was doing. Some infants are that way – they laugh before they know what they're about and it scares them quite out of their little baby wits. Emma's first laugh came when she was finger-painting (with apple sauce). It was part "*Hah!*" and part "*Hic!*" She was so scared of her own laugh that she didn't giggle again until she was walking. (Ask your parents sometime what your first laugh sounded like. If you were a "*Hah! Hic!*" perhaps your laugh gave birth to a fairy like Avery.)

"Avery's teachers gave up on her," said Caraway Cooke in the silent kitchen, "and sent her here to work in the kitchen when she was tiny. A serving

fairy is what she'll be all her life. For the likes of Claudine and Amanda." Caraway sniffed.

"They gave up on you?" Lily couldn't imagine such a thing. She thought of Faith and her fairy school. Faith would never give up on any of her students! Especially not Lily! "That's terrible!" she said.

"Isn't that how it is on Sheepskerry?"

"No!" said Lily. "On Sheepskerry, the teachers know that every fairy is good at different things. Not every fairy learns the same way."

"You'd better not let the mainland fairies hear you talk that way," said Avery.

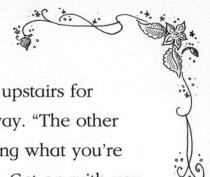

"And you'd best get upstairs for breakfast," said Caraway. "The other fairies will be wondering what you're doing talking to Avery. Get on with you, now. And don't come back."

Chapter Twelve

*L*ily could barely concentrate as she went upstairs to breakfast. The other fairies were talking in high-pitched, excited voices and flitting about the breakfast table. They were chattering so loudly that they didn't notice how quiet Lily was.

The single topic of conversation was what this year's fancy-dress theme would be.

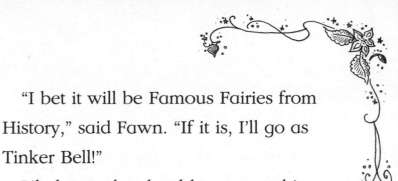

"I bet it will be Famous Fairies from History," said Fawn. "If it is, I'll go as Tinker Bell!"

Lily knew she should say something about her famous sister, but she was too lost in thought to say a word.

"I hope it's Magic Animals," said a fairy named Arabella. She was a mainland fairy and seemed much kinder than the Townley sisters. "I would be a magical unicorn."

The other fairies chimed in.

"And I'd be a dragon!"

"And I'd be a phoenix with rainbow wings!"

"It's no use guessing," said Claudine. "We won't know what the theme is until

Queen Titania's letter arrives."

Lily's mind was still on Avery. "The unfairness of it all!" she said out loud.

The fairies were silent.

"Lily Bell?" said Amanda. "Are you saying our queen is unfair?"

"Your queen?" said Lily. She was embarrassed that she had not been following the conversation.

"Queen Titania sends us a letter announcing the costume theme on the morning of the party," said Amanda, as if Lily were a simpleton. "Then we observe a code of fairy silence until all the costumes are made."

"That's the way it has always been done," said Claudine. "And the way we'll do it this year – even with you island fairies here. There's nothing unfair about it."

"Oh, I didn't mean—"

There was a sharp knock at the front door.

"Queen Titania's page!"

A young fairy in a smart gold outfit arrived on the doorstep of Amanda and Claudine's house. She presented Amanda with a scroll.

All the fairies gathered around the
letter with great excitement.

"Remember! Silence from now on,"
said Amanda. She unrolled the scroll
and hung it up on the wall behind her.

Lily just hoped that the costume theme
would be something perfect for her. *But
whatever it is*, she thought, *I'll do my best
for Sheepskerry.*

When she looked at the scroll,
her face fell. It was in very fancy
handwriting. It must have been written
by Queen Titania herself!

None of the fairies made a sound.
Lily looked up at the wall of words and
did what Faith told her to do. She took
a deep breath and focused her eyes on

the swirling words, one at a time. But still the letters pushed together and the words floated around the page. She could only make out a word here and there.

nature

MAGICAL

fairies

Dress

help

Where was Clara, who read to her every night? Or Rosie, who would have whispered every word written on the scroll? Where was Silver, who'd say the code of silence was silly and everyone should help one another?

Lily's wings were shaking and she was sure her face was as pale as birch bark. What if she did not know what kind of costume she was to wear to the party?

The fairies began to float away, one by one, all with great grins on their faces. Soon only Claudine was left. Lily took a break from trying to read the scroll. She looked over at Claudine for a moment.

"Whatever's the matter, Lily Bell?"

Claudine whispered.

Lily shook her head. She did not want to break the code of silence!

"Queen Titania won't mind if we talk a little now," said Claudine. "The competition doesn't start officially until the Magical Treasure Chest arrives."

"Truly?" asked Lily.

"Truly," said Claudine. "Honest."

"It's just that—"

"You have trouble reading, don't you, Lily?" said Claudine.

It was the first time it felt hard to reply to that question. "Yes," she said. "I do."

If Lily had not been looking down at her sweet little red boots, she might have seen a very small smile cross Claudine's face. "Not to worry," Claudine told Lily. "Here. Let me read it to you."

Claudine turned to face the scroll on the wall. This is what she told Lily it said:

"Titania, Queen of the Mainland,
does hereby announce and decree
that each fairy attending the
FANCY-DRESS PARTY
shall create her own costume
(in silence with no help from others),
using seven items from
QUEEN TITANIA'S MAGICAL
COSTUME TRUNK
and elements from nature.
Each fairy
shall dress in the manner of a
WITCH."

Claudine paused. "Got that, Lily?" she asked.

"Got it," said Lily. "Thank you, Claudine! Thank you so much. I'll make the best witch costume ever."

Claudine smiled. "You do that, Lily Bell," she said. "And may the best fairy win."

Chapter Thirteen

Precisely one hour later, Queen Titania's Magical Costume Trunk appeared in the Townley sisters' parlour in a puff of sparkling smoke and all the fairies gathered around to wait for it to open.

"One at a time!" called Amanda. "I'm first. The rest of you get behind me."

Lily was dying to push her way to the front so she could have her pick of the

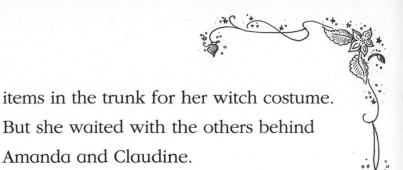

items in the trunk for her witch costume. But she waited with the others behind Amanda and Claudine.

"You were last to breakfast this morning, Lily," said Amanda. "So all of us think you should be last in line, don't we, fairies?"

The other fairies said nothing.

"I suppose that's fair," said Lily, though she wasn't convinced.

The magical trunk opened with a peal of fairy bells. Lily waited and waited as all the other fairies floated up to the trunk and flew away with their choices. *I hope there are a* few *good things left for me!* she thought. Finally Fawn Deere flew out with a wink to Lily. She had

chosen an armful of pink and sparkly
items, which Lily thought was rather
odd, considering the witchy theme. But
she didn't have time to think about it. It
was her turn to choose.

The magical trunk was a massive old leather box, but it crackled and sparkled and it was packed with bits and pieces that would be perfect for costume making. Even after a dozen other fairies had taken their share of pieces, it was still full to the brim.

A treasure trove of jewels and shiny skirts and a pair of white opera gloves lay on top of the pile. Lily looked at them longingly and since she couldn't resist, she tried them on. "How beautiful I would look if I went to the party in those lovely things!" she sighed as she gazed in a little mirror. "But they're not for this witch!"

Just underneath a pair of pink tights,

Lily was a little surprised to find a roll
of black taffeta and a length of deep
purple lace. And under that, she spotted
a shiny pointed hat and an old crooked
broom.

"Perfect!" she said. "I can't believe the
other fairies left these for me!" She put
her four choices aside. Now she had
three more.

She chose some scuffed black slippers
and a length of shimmering silk chiffon.
Then she spotted a make-up kit. "Whoa-
ho!" she said. "I can give myself green
skin with this! And a warty nose!"

Lily considered herself in the mirror
that hung over the parlour fireplace. She
peered in close and turned her head so

she could see her charming profile. "I imagine the other fairies don't dare look too witchy," she said, "but I'm not afraid. I want to be the best witch the mainland has ever seen and if it means I grow a warty nose, then a warty nose it will be!"

Chapter Fourteen

All that afternoon, Lily worked on her costume. She trimmed the pointy hat with sea urchins she had brought from Sheepskerry's west shore. She snipped and stitched and made the roll of black taffeta into a swirling cape lined with purple lace and sewed deep blue mussel shells on the collar. "Reversible!" Lily exclaimed with delight as she tried it on.

Her gown was made of sheer black

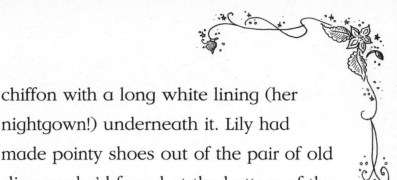

chiffon with a long white lining (her nightgown!) underneath it. Lily had made pointy shoes out of the pair of old slippers she'd found at the bottom of the costume box and she painted her best white tights with red stripes.

Lily's costume was almost done when there was a knock at the door. Avery peeked her head inside.

"Can I come in?" she asked. Then she started in surprise. "Oh! I'm sorry. I thought this was Lily's room!"

Lily burst into laughter.

"Oh, it is you!" cried Avery. "I didn't even recognise you when I came in. You look *horrible*!"

Lily didn't want to break the code

of silence, but she gave Avery a gap-
toothed grin.

"You can talk to me, Lily. I'm not in
the contest!"

"Phew!" said Lily. "It's so good to
talk at last! I'm just going to put some
cobwebs on my wings and then I'll be
done," she said. "Lucky thing I brought
those cobwebs from Sheepskerry!" She
had to twist sideways to get the right
effect. "Don't help me! I don't want to
cheat!" She draped some stringy webs on
her wingtips. "How are the other fairies
doing?" she asked, hoping they were not
quite as witchy as she was.

"I haven't seen anyone else," said
Avery. "All their doors are closed. And I

only wanted to see *you*!"

Lily glued one more wart on her nose. "Time to go!" she said. "How do I look?"

"You are the scariest witch I have ever seen!"

Lily spun around and looked at herself in the mirror every way she could.

"If I'm not the ugliest witch at this fancy-dress party," she said, "I'll eat my pointy hat!"

Chapter Fifteen

*T*he clock on the mantelpiece chimed six times.

Lily opened the door to her room and peered out into the hallway. "I wonder where all the other fairies are," she said. "I'm not late, am I?"

"No," said Avery. "You're right on time."

"They must already have gathered in the entrance hall. Come on, let's hurry!"

114

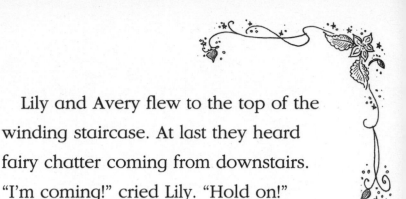

Lily and Avery flew to the top of the winding staircase. At last they heard fairy chatter coming from downstairs. "I'm coming!" cried Lily. "Hold on!"

When Lily spoke, the fairy chatter died down. Lily didn't notice the quiet, though; she was so excited to make her entrance. She closed her eyes at the top of the staircase. It was all just as she had dreamed it would be. "Here I am!" she called. "I fly for Sheepskerry and Queen Mab!"

There was a moment of absolute silence. Lily's eyes popped open. And then… there was an enormous burst of laughter.

"She's a witch!"

"She's hideous!"
"Didn't she read the letter?"
"Look! She's got warts on her nose!"

If Lily's face had not been green, the
other fairies would have seen her cheeks
turn scarlet from humiliation and shame.
If the brim of her hat had not hidden her
eyes, the other fairies would have seen
tears welling up in them. And if any of
the other fairies had noticed the broom
she was sitting on, they would have seen
it shaking.

"Oh, Lily! Fly away!" cried Avery behind her. "Don't you see? They tricked you!"

Shall I tell you now what Queen Titania's invitation really said? Or have you already guessed? If you have, your heart will have gone out to dear, trusting Lily.

Here's the invitation, and it *is* quite tricky to read. You can read it yourself or you can ask someone to read it for you, if you'd prefer. I do so hope that where you're reading this is not like the fairy mainland. I do so hope that you have a friend or a sister or a teacher like Faith!

Titania, Queen of the Mainland,
does hereby announce and decree
that each fairy attending the
FANCY-DRESS PARTY
shall create her own costume
(in silence with no help from others),
using seven items from
QUEEN TITANIA'S
MAGICAL COSTUME TRUNK
and elements from nature.
Each fairy
shall dress in the manner of a
PRINCESS.

Poor, poor Lily!

Every single other fairy was adorned from head to toe in tulle and silk and lace, and every part of it was pink. They carried ruby wands and wore diamond tiaras and capes of purest pearl satin. Their shoes were trimmed with feathers and their hair was piled on top of their heads in beautiful cascading curls. And every fairy's wings were sprinkled with sparkles.

"What's the matter, Lily Bell?" asked Claudine. "Is this how princesses look on Sheepskerry Island?"

Lily held absolutely still. She felt as if her witch's dress were sucking all the breath out of her. She wished her broomstick would break into two so she

could sink into the floor. She wanted
to fly away from this horrible mainland
and never come back. But more than
anything, she wanted to punch Claudine
Townley on the nose.

She did none of these things.

Lily Bell hitched her broomstick under
her, straightened her pointy hat, and
flew right down into that cloud of pink
fairy princesses.

"What are you waiting for?" she said.
"Let's go."

Chapter Sixteen

Off they flew.

It was a long way to Queen Titania's castle.

Lily's mood, very bleak when she started the flight, lightened as she travelled. She couldn't help herself: she loved flying in the fresh evening air. And she had never travelled on a broomstick! The beating of her wings and the wind in her hair gave her new energy. *I will*

122

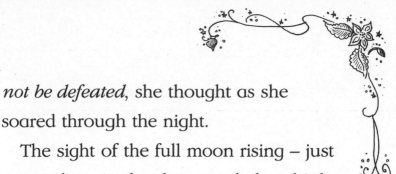

not be defeated, she thought as she
soared through the night.

The sight of the full moon rising – just
a tiny sliver in the sky – made her think
of moonrise on Sheepskerry and of her
sisters waiting for her at home. *What
would my sisters do?*

Sensible Clara would take off the
green make-up and warts, change into
comfy pyjamas and go right to bed, the
thought of the party far behind her. *Well,
that's out*, thought Lily.

Rosie would forgive Claudine and
Amanda, imagining that the Townley
sisters must be very unhappy themselves
if they could do such an unkind thing
to someone else. Then she would go to

the party and applaud when someone else won the prize. *That's* really *out*, Lily thought.

Silver would fly into the fancy-dress party with Squeakie squeaking in her arms and announce to Queen Titania that there were some very mean fairies on the mainland. Then she'd enjoy herself quite happily as a witch. *That's not me, either*, thought Lily.

A lovely length of grapevine caught her eye as she flew. She swooped down to pick it up from the ground where it had fallen.

Lily heard someone flying nearby. It was Fawn and she looked absolutely stricken.

124

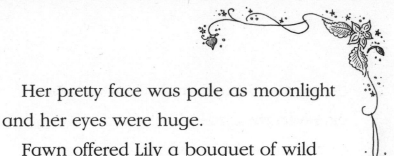

Her pretty face was pale as moonlight and her eyes were huge.

Fawn offered Lily a bouquet of wild white roses. "I picked these for you in the park."

Lily took them without a word.

"I'm sorry, Lily. I didn't know. None of us knew you'd dress like that."

Lily did not believe that for a second.

"You didn't know that Claudine was going to trick me?"

"We didn't! We didn't!" cried Fawn. "I mean, we knew that she would make you choose last – but we only went along with it because you're so inventive! I feel ashamed now, but then I just thought it would give us a little help. I didn't know Claudine told you to be a witch! Nobody knew that!"

"Except maybe Amanda," said Lily.

Fawn nodded her head in dismay. "Yes," she said. "Except maybe Amanda." She looked into Lily's green face. "What are you going to do, Lily?" she asked. "Are you really going to go to the fancy-dress party like that? I suppose

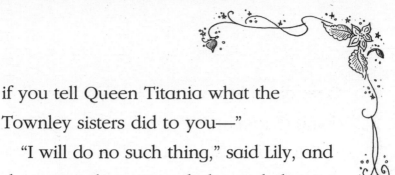

if you tell Queen Titania what the
Townley sisters did to you—"

"I will do no such thing," said Lily, and
she scooped up some dark purple leaves
from the path below. She had a plan
in the back of her mind, although she
wasn't quite sure what it was. "Claudine
and Amanda played a trick on me. Now I
will play a trick on them."

"Oh, don't, Lily! Please don't make this
any worse than it already is."

Lily just smiled. "Don't worry, Fawn,"
she said. She plucked a handful of lacy
white flowers from the roadside. "My
trick will be perfectly fair. And it may
even teach those fairies a lesson. You
wait and see."

Chapter Seventeen

*L*ily's keen eye spotted a few more things to pick up as she flew to the castle. If she had not been so excited about her plan, she would have spent a little more time being amazed at the castle when they arrived there. It was unlike anything she'd ever seen – even Queen Mab's Palace on Sheepskerry was nothing compared to this! The castle was made of stone, not twigs and leaves, and it was as high as

a boulder. Turrets and towers rose from
its walls. A drawbridge was let down as
the fairies entered. Royal swans paddled
in the moat. And the place was lit from
top to bottom with firefly lanterns on
the outside and beeswax candles on the
inside. What a marvel!

"Shall we wait together until we're called into the ballroom, Lily?" asked Fawn Deere. She was very loyal under the circumstances. For what fairy princess would want to enter a party with a witch?

"No, Fawn, I'm fine," said Lily. "I'm just going to make a stop in the little fairies' room and re-do my face."

Fawn kissed Lily on the cheek. "You're very brave, Lily Bell."

"Not so very brave – but I do have some excellent ideas," said Lily and she flew off down the long hall to find the little fairies' room. She hoped it would be empty.

It was.

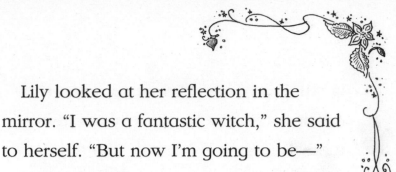

Lily looked at her reflection in the mirror. "I was a fantastic witch," she said to herself. "But now I'm going to be—"

"Oh, Lily! What are you going to be?" Avery burst through the door. "It's too late to change your costume!"

"Avery! What are you doing here?"

"I told Queen Titania I would work at the party," said Avery, "because I wanted to be here with you!"

Lily rushed over and hugged her dear new friend. "I'm so glad you're here, Avery," she said. "You can hold my hand as I make myself into a princess!"

"But how will you do that when you're a witch?" asked Avery.

Lily was pulling the warts off her

nose. "Ouch!" she exclaimed. Then she grinned. "Not every princess has to be a pink princess," she said. "I'm going to this fancy-dress party as the Princess of the Night." She scrubbed the green face paint off and her rosy cheeks shone with excitement. "Just you watch me!"

Then she emptied her pockets. Out fell the vine leaves, the delicate lacy white flowers and some gorgeous dark feathers. She flipped her cape inside out and threaded the ruby leaves through the purple lace. She twisted the white roses around the vine leaves to make a crown. She shook the cobwebs off her wings. They seemed to sparkle all on their own.

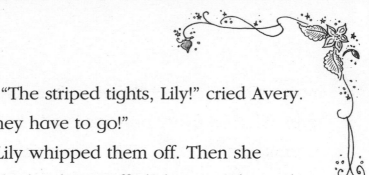

"The striped tights, Lily!" cried Avery. "They have to go!"

Lily whipped them off. Then she looked at her scuffed slippers. She tied Fawn's white roses on them; the evening dew made them shine.

"Is that it?" asked Lily. "Am I ready to go?"

"You've forgotten to get rid of your witch's hair!" cried Avery, laughing. "Even a princess of the night brushes her hair!"

Lily shook her head and started to untangle the mess she'd made of her long, golden hair. She combed out the snarls and brushed her hair until it shone. Then Avery placed the crown on her head.

"Now," said Avery, "you are beautiful. Stay still for one minute and I'll sketch a portrait!" Avery took a pencil and a tiny sketchpad from her pocket and with a few swift lines she drew a lovely likeness of her new friend.

"Oh!" cried Lily. "It's beautiful!"

Just then the queen's swans sounded

their fanfare.

"It's time for the costume judging!" said Avery. "Hurry! This is it!"

Lily gave Avery a quick hug; then the two fairies flew back towards the Great Hall. All the other fairies were gathered behind a curtain, waiting to be called by Queen Titania. One by one they flew into the hall to meet with the queen.

Lily drew the curtain aside just a little so she could see what was going on. Amanda Townley was breathtakingly beautiful in a knee-length ballerina skirt and a diamond tiara. Claudine was even more elegant in a glorious ball gown with a deep rose-coloured bow. Fawn and the other fairies were gorgeous too,

even if it was a little hard to tell them apart.

"I don't mind who wins or loses now," said Lily to herself. "I'm just proud to have done my best." She lifted her chin and waited for her name to be called. Her wings were quivering, but even Lily couldn't tell whether they trembled from excitement or fear.

Chapter Eighteen

*L*ily heard the voice of the queen's lady-in-waiting. "Fawn Deere is the last fairy to compete in the fancy-dress party," she said, checking her list, "as Amanda Townley has informed me that Lily Bell will not be—"

Lily burst out of her hiding place. "Here I am!" she cried, this time with her eyes wide open. "Lily Crystal Bell, Princess of the Night, flying for

Sheepskerry Island and Queen Mab!"

Gone was the hideous witch the fairies were expecting. Before them flew a glorious princess in deepest shades of midnight with a cape festooned with autumn leaves and a coronet of white roses.

Lily fluttered before Queen Titania's throne. "Lily Bell of Sheepskerry," said the queen in her deep voice. "Is this your idea of a princess?"

"It is, Your Majesty." Lily rubbed her nose with her sleeve, hoping she'd taken off all the green make-up. "I am a dark princess and a good princess."

"That is quite an original idea," said Queen Titania. She leaned close to Lily.

"You may not know this, but I was a princess of the night myself. A dark princess. And a good princess. Like you." Then she added in a whisper, "Ask Queen Mab about it. We grew up together, you know."

Lily beamed.

"Fairies," said Queen Titania, "who will our costume winner be tonight?"

Avery was the first to cheer. "Lily!" she cried. "It should be Lily Bell!"

The fairy princesses were quiet for a moment. Then Fawn Deere's applause joined Avery's. Soon all the fairies were cheering. "Hooray! Hooray for Lily!"

"Stop it!" cried Claudine Townley.

"Stop it at once!" shouted Amanda. But no one paid them any attention.

"Li-ly!" the fairies cried. "*Li-ly!* LI-LY! LI-LY!" All the fairies – with the exception of two – were calling Lily's name.

Lily curtsied low before Queen Titania (and she noticed, out of the corner of

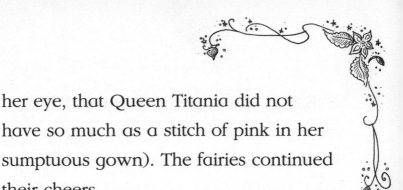

her eye, that Queen Titania did not
have so much as a stitch of pink in her
sumptuous gown). The fairies continued
their cheers.

"Lily Bell of Sheepskerry," said Queen
Titania, "the fairies have declared you
the clear winner. And not even a queen
would disagree with them."

Queen Titania's
enchanted black
cat brought in
the prize – a
golden medal on a
ribbon of purple velvet,
which matched Lily's outfit perfectly.

"I like your mussel shells," said
Queen Titania in a whisper. Then she

declared, "This is for you, Lily Bell, and for all of Sheepskerry. Take it with my blessing." She turned to the other fairies. "And now, fairy princesses, it is time to celebrate *all* your achievements at our fancy-dress party."

"May the festivities commence!" cried the queen's lady-in-waiting.

The party lasted deep into the night and Lily was the belle of the ball.

Chapter Nineteen

*D*awn came far too soon the next morning, but Lily didn't really mind. She had packed up her bags the night before. She was eager to go home. Avery had promised she'd meet her at the dock to say goodbye. How long ago it seemed since she'd first arrived on the mainland! And how much had happened!

Silently she flew down to the big wooden door of the Townleys' fairy town house. Her bags did not seem so heavy now. "Goodbye, Claudine and Amanda," she said. "You gave me a rough ride."

She was just about to slip outside when she saw an envelope on the front table. It was addressed, in very clear writing, *to Lily Crystal Bell.*

Inside was a letter, which she took her time to read.

Dear Lily,

We're sorry we were so mean to you this weekend. And that Claudine tricked you into dressing as a witch for the fancy-dress party. We won't do it again. Come back soon (and tell us how you

made that leafy cape!).
Your friends, maybe?
Amanda and Claudine

"*Humph,*" said Lily. "I wonder if they mean it." She picked up the letter and tucked it in her shoe bag. "I'll just have to come back to see if they do."

Lily's sparrow carriage was waiting for her as she left the town house. The chipper little sparrow took her straight down to the dock.

"I guess Avery slept in today, not that I blame her." Lily sighed. "I will miss her so much when I get back home." The glimmer of an idea shone in the back of her mind, but she didn't quite know what she was thinking. Then she heard the squawk of her sparrow carriage driver.

"We're here already!"

The ferry dock was silent and empty when Lily arrived. But she was right on time. She could just see Merryweather's nose poking out of the water as the faithful grey seal paddled towards the shore.

Suddenly she heard a rush of wings.

"You made it, Avery!" cried Lily.

"Of course I did!" said Avery.

"How will we ever get along without each other?" said Lily. "I wish you could come to Sheepskerry. Then we could see each other every day!"

"Oh, I wish I could!" said Avery.

Merryweather gave three short barks.
Suddenly Lily realised exactly what her
idea was.

"But… you *could* go with me, Avery,"

she said. "You could come to the island. You would love it on Sheepskerry. And you wouldn't have to be a serving fairy there."

Avery's face lit up for a second. But then the light dimmed. "How could I leave Caraway Cooke? And my duties in the town house?"

"Caraway's sister could work in the kitchen."

"It's true," said Avery. "She's asked for that a million times."

"Then let her take your place. Oh, you can be a Sheepskerry fairy! And you could live with us. Or..."

Suddenly, Lily remembered Faith's voice: *How I would love a little*

companionship, now that winter is drawing near.

"Faith Learned will take care of you! Her sisters are all gone."

In an instant, the two fairies had settled everything. While Merryweather played in the bay, Avery sent a homing-pigeon message to Caraway Cooke. She drew a special message to let Caraway know where she was going and asked her to send along her things. She promised she would write (or draw) a note every week.

"And now," said Lily, "there's only one thing left to do."

"What's that?" asked Avery.

"To say: let's be best friends."

"Yes!" cried Avery, and threw her arms around Lily. "Let's be best friends."

Merryweather barked again. The tide was turning.

"Time to go!" said Lily. She jumped aboard. "Coming?"

"Coming," said Avery.

As the sun rose and Merryweather
paddled towards the distant shore, Lily
held Avery's hand. "What a lot we will
have to tell my sisters!" she said. Then
she turned and looked behind her.
"Goodbye, mainland," she said. "Thanks
for my very first – solo! – adventure. I'll
be back again. Pretty soon."

FAIRY SECRETS

Squeak's Words

Yo-ca! – Me too!

Ma-bo-bo – I love you.

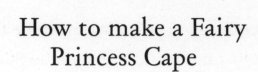

How to make a Fairy Princess Cape

This is a perfect project for a rainy day. You'll need a grown-up to help!

What you'll need:

A large piece of cloth from a Magical Costume Trunk. If you do not have a Magical Costume Trunk, then you'll need to buy a piece of fabric from a fabric shop or perhaps you have something at home that you could use.

A long piece of ribbon to tie your cape approx. 1.5 metres long.

Fabric glue or a sewing machine (or a needle and thread if you're the Stitch sisters).

Decorations – feathers, felt flowers, ribbons, glitter glue or anything you like.

How to make the cape:
Cut the piece of fabric so that it makes the kind of cape you'd like to wear. It can be a square or a rectangle or a semicircle. Whatever you like best.

Place the ribbon along the top of the fabric, about 2 centimetres below the fabric's edge.

Squeeze a thick line of fabric glue along the edge of the fabric below the ribbon.

Fold the edge of the fabric over the ribbon to create a hem, being careful not to touch the ribbon with the glue.

Let the glue dry. (If you sew the hem instead, there's no drying time!)

Decorate the outside of the cape with the decorations. And if your cape is reversible, decorate the inside too.

Have you read
Silver and Rosie's adventures?

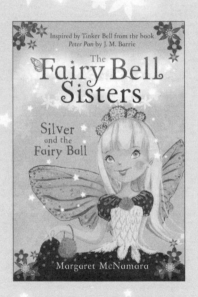
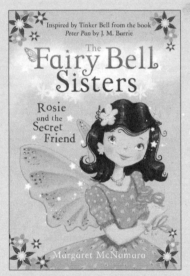